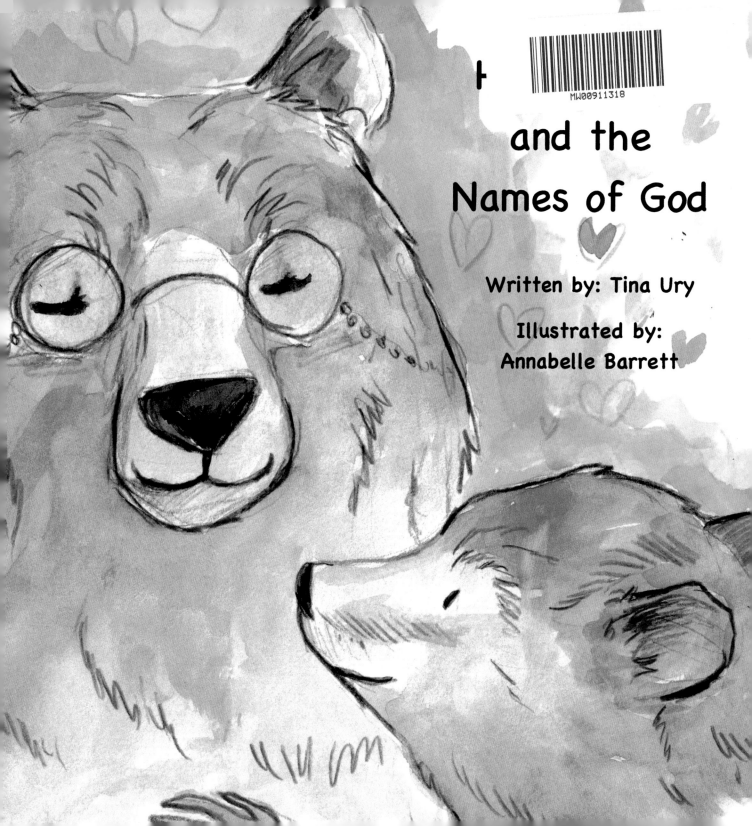

and the
Names of God

Written by: Tina Ury

Illustrated by:
Annabelle Barrett

Today, Honey Bear, let's talk about the Names of God.

Who is GOD, Baba?

GOD is the Being who was, who is, and who will always be. He is always there and He is good.

Names are important because they help describe the person you are talking about. We are known by our names, little one. I call you Honey Bear because you are SOOO sweet. You call me Baba, but others might say Grandma, GG, or even Nana. Elohim, or God, has many names He is known by too!

God's name, YAHWEH, is the name that holds great power and authority.
It means "THE LORD".

God is the one and only CREATOR.
What is a CREATOR, Baba?

The CREATOR is the one that made all living things, like the mountains, forests, flowers, sunshine, and even you Honey Bear!

Everything comes from Him, exists by His power and is intended for His glory. All glory to Him forever. (Rom 11:36)

Did you know that EL ROI is the name of GOD WHO SEES? What does GOD see, Baba?

God is sooooo big that He sees EVERYTHING all at once. Nowhere can you hide from Him.

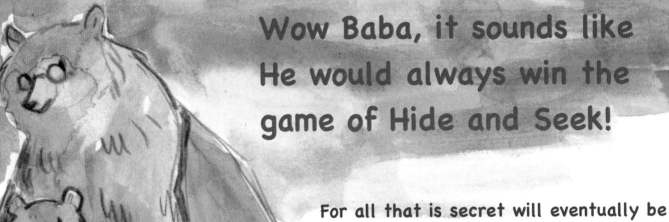

Wow Baba, it sounds like He would always win the game of Hide and Seek!

For all that is secret will eventually be brought into the open, and everything concealed will be brought to light and made known to all. (Luke 8:17)

The Lord is also called our SHEPHERD.

What's a SHEPHERD, Baba?

A SHEPHERD is a PROTECTOR of sheep. He shows them the way to safety. The sheep hear and know His voice and they follow Him.

Is it kinda like Follow the Leader, Baba?

Did you know God is also known as JESUS?

Who is JESUS?   JESUS is God's only Son, who was sent to earth from heaven. He lived a perfect life so that you can know more about God and His great love for you.

JESUS was and still is the very best friend you could have!

For God so loved the world: He gave His one and only Son, so that whoever believes in Him will have eternal life. (John 3:16)

JESUS is called the SAVIOR of the world. What's a SAVIOR?

The SAVIOR saves you from danger and darkness. He even shows you how to stay free from it.

Like a super hero, Baba?

Did you know that GOD is also called AGAPE LOVE?

What is AGAPE LOVE, Baba?

AGAPE LOVE is the highest form of love anyone can have. It is a selfless, kind, unconditional love.

AGAPE loves you when you are good or bad, no matter what! Isn't that good news Honey Bear?

You AGAPE LOVE me, don't you, Baba?

This is my commandment, that you love one another as I have loved you. (John 15:12-13)

Another name for God is JEHOVAH JIREH, which means your PROVIDER.

What is a PROVIDER, Baba?

Our PROVIDER gives us what we need in life, and He gives many gifts we want as well. That can be really fun!

Is it like Christmas morning, Baba?

Every good gift comes from above (James 1:17)

Another of God's many names is EL ELYON, which means God Most High.

He is bigger than any problem we might face in this world! You can trust Him! He is our hope! What is HOPE, Baba? It is the person, place or thing you put your trust in, Honey Bear.

Is it like when you wish for something upon a star and you hope for it to come true?

Yes, Honey, but when God is your HOPE, you believe in your heart that HE can be trusted in ALL things.

God's source of hope, will fill you completely with joy and peace, with a confident hope through the Power of the Holy Spirit. (Rom 15:14)

...which means, PEACE OF GOD!

What is PEACE OF GOD, Baba?

That is the feeling in your heart of calm and quiet in a world that can be very loud and crazy sometimes.

God gives my heart peace when we snuggle, Baba!

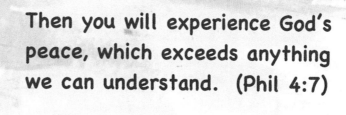

Then you will experience God's peace, which exceeds anything we can understand. (Phil 4:7)

Did you know that God is called the LIVING WORD, Honey Bear?

What is the LIVING WORD, Baba?

All scripture is breathed out by God and profitable for teaching in righteousness. (2 Tim 3:16)

The LIVING WORD is a name for the Bible. The Bible is a book full of encouragement and instructions that tells us more about who God is. It helps us live a life that pleases God.

There are lots of wonderful mysteries to discover in the Bible. It is also known as the greatest love story ever!

Baba, that sounds like a map that shows us the way to the treasure!

Did you know that God is called ABBA in HEAVEN?

What is ABBA and what is HEAVEN?

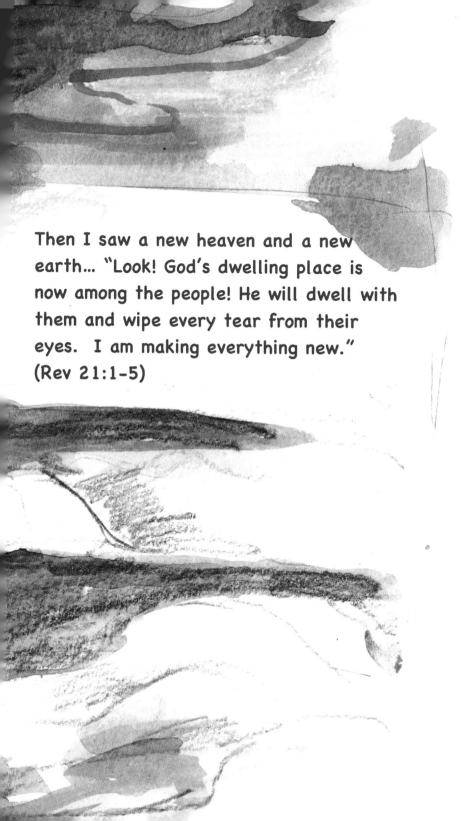

Then I saw a new heaven and a new earth... "Look! God's dwelling place is now among the people! He will dwell with them and wipe every tear from their eyes. I am making everything new." (Rev 21:1-5)

ABBA is a loving name for HEAVENLY FATHER.

HEAVEN is a beautiful place where He lives.

ABBA wants us to live there with Him forever someday.

Did you know that when you make Jesus your Savior, He gives you the HOLY SPIRIT who then lives inside of you?

What's the HOLY SPIRIT, Baba?

The HOLY SPIRIT is our HELPER in all things. He gives us the power to love God and love people the way HE loves us! Doesn't God have many amazing names to help us know him better Honey Bear?

Yes, and I want to know more about him, He sounds awesome!

The Advocate, the Holy Spirit, whom the Father will send in my name will teach you all things and will remind you of everything I have said to you. (John 14:26)

Let's pray and talk with God, Honey Bear, and thank Him for His many names!

God wants so much, to have a personal relationship with you. He wants to show you He is a good Father who loves you more than you will ever understand. He wants you to know that He sent Jesus, His only Son, to shed His blood, die on the cross, and then be raised from the dead. He did all that so that you can be set free from the bondage of sin, the fear of death, and enter into eternal life. He did it so you can have hope on this earth. He wants you to get to know Him, His names, His character, and His Son through the Bible and the power of the Holy Spirit living in you. He is calling you to be a follower of Jesus Christ. Will you make that decision?

Salvation Prayer – If you want to become a follower of Jesus, pray this prayer:

Jesus, I change my mind about You. You are the Son of God, You are the Christ and You are Lord. You came into this world to show us the way we are to live and to provide eternal life to those who would accept You.

I believe in my heart that God raised You from the dead and You are alive forevermore, seated on Your throne in heaven next to the Father. I confess my sins to You and ask You to forgive them. I receive You as my personal Lord, King and Savior. I invite You, Jesus, to have first place in my heart. I no longer choose to be in charge of my life, I give it to You. I believe Your blood, that was shed on the cross washes away all my sin. Come now and make me clean. Restore me to a right relationship as a child of my Heavenly Father.

 Thank You Lord, for your cleansing blood! I now stand clean in Your presence. I put on Your robe of righteousness, which You are handing to me. Thank You, Lord. Amen!

You are now a follower of Christ! Praise Him!

"To all who received Him, to those who believed in His name, He gave the right to become children of God" (John 1:11-12)

Made in the USA
Lexington, KY
23 October 2019